GREEN WILMA

GREEN WILMA

Tedd Arnold

Dial Books for Young Readers New York

For Imogene,
Wilma, and
Green Dog

Published by Dial Books for Young Readers
A Division of Penguin Books USA Inc.
375 Hudson Street
New York, New York 10014

Copyright © 1993 by Tedd Arnold
All rights reserved
Design by Nancy R. Leo
Printed in Hong Kong
by South China Printing Company (1988) Limited
First Edition
1 3 5 7 9 10 8 6 4 2

Library of Congress Cataloging in Publication Data
Arnold, Tedd.
Green Wilma / by Tedd Arnold.—1st ed.
p.   cm.
Summary: Waking up with a frog-like appearance, Wilma proves
disruptive at school as she searches for some tasty flies.
ISBN 0-8037-1313-4—ISBN 0-8037-1314-2 (lib.)
[1. Frogs—Fiction. 2. Schools—Fiction. 3. Stories in rhyme.]
I. Title.
PZ8.3.A647GR 1993   [E]—dc20   91-31501   CIP   AC

The artwork was prepared using color pencils and watercolor
washes. It was then color-separated and reproduced as red,
blue, yellow, and black halftones.

One morning Wilma woke up green, and
much to her surprise

She sat up on her bed and croaked and
started eating flies.

She washed, she dressed, she combed her hair,
she quickly made her bed.

She hopped down to the breakfast table.
"Pass the bugs," she said.

"Green children should not go to school,"
she heard her mother fuss.

But out the window Wilma jumped and
rode off on the bus.

In class Green Wilma tried but simply
couldn't keep her seat.

In gym while playing dodgeball Wilma
never could be beat.

In art the kids thought being green was
absolutely great!

But Teacher said, "The green must be from
something that she ate."

At story time poor Wilma felt so
hungry she could cry.

And then she saw on Teacher's nose a
tasty little fly.

She chased it all around the room and
up and down the hall,

And through the lunchroom (that's the place that
flies love best of all).

The principal yelled, "Stop her! She should
know we have a rule

That children aren't allowed to munch on
flies while they're in school."

Then out the door Green Wilma hopped,
into the hills beyond,

And finally she caught that fly
up over Miller's Pond.

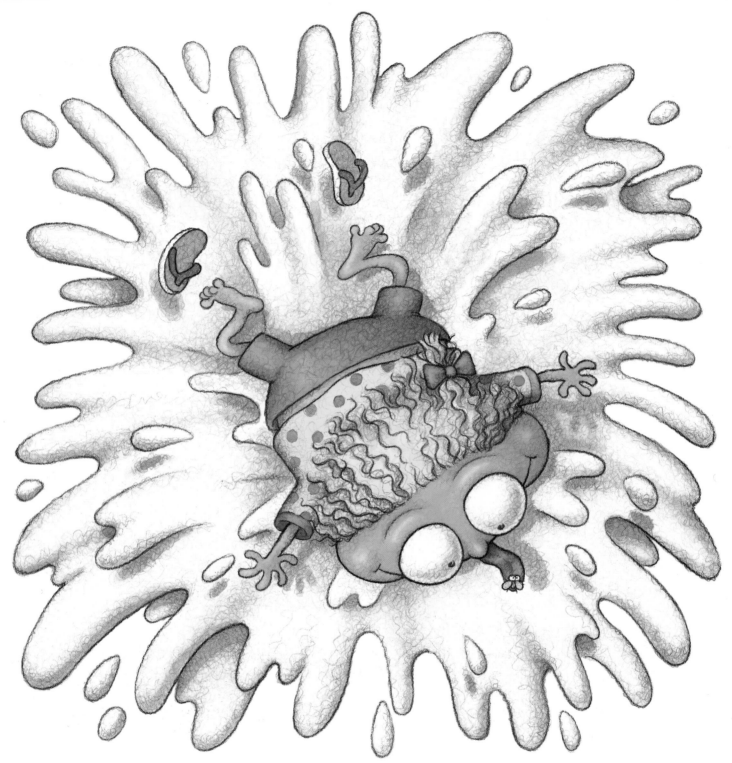

Wilma landed in the water
with a noisy splash,

She met a very hungry fish...

and woke up in a flash.

Then she recalled the words they teach to
every little frog,

"When you dream, be careful that you
don't fall off the log."

DATE			